The Wind in the Willows

Retold by

Samantha Noonan

Illustrated by

Vince Reid

ARCTURUS

To Dad, remembering many happy evenings
reading about the Riverbank—SN.

For Lucia and Ronan—VR.

This edition published in 2018 by Arcturus Publishing Limited
26/27 Bickels Yard, 151–153 Bermondsey Street,
London SE1 3HA

Writer: Samantha Noonan
Illustrator: Vince Reid
Designer: Jeni Child
Editor: Becca Clunes
Art Director: Jessica Crass

ISBN: 978-1-78828-696-1
CH006286NT
Supplier 24, Date 0318, Print run 6736

Printed in Malaysia

Contents

CHAPTER 1

The Summertime River...........................4

CHAPTER 2

The Wild Wood 14

CHAPTER 3

Toad's Lesson.......................................24

CHAPTER 4

A Grand Escape...................................34

CHAPTER 5

Homeward Bound 44

CHAPTER 6

The Battle for Toad Hall 54

CHAPTER 1

The Summertime River

There once was a mole who lived underground. One day, he was spring-cleaning his house. It was hard work, and when he paused for a moment, he felt something calling to him from above the ground—something light and exciting. It was the call of spring! Mole threw down his duster and started to burrow upward through the earth until his pink nose popped into bright sunlight.

He rolled out into the warm grass of

 a meadow. It was so golden and pleasant above the ground! Birds were

singing, flowers were blooming, and
across the meadow was something Mole
had never seen before: a river!

As Mole stared at the water, a
Water Rat came rowing along
in a smart little blue-
and-white boat.

"Hello, there!"
said the Rat, noticing Mole gazing at him.
"Would you like to come aboard?"

"Oh, yes, please!" cried Mole.

Rat rowed over to him, and Mole
carefully climbed in. They glided off
down the river.

"This is wonderful," said Mole, leaning
back, "I've never been in a boat before!"

"What, *never*?" exclaimed Rat. "Why,
I think there is nothing better than
messing about in boats!"

"I think I like boats already," said Mole, waggling his back paws.

"Well, then, let's spend a day on the river!" replied Rat.

He rowed them downstream, tied the boat up to the bank, and pulled out a picnic basket. Inside was the most wonderful picnic Mole had ever seen! There were cold meats, pickles, egg sandwiches, and salad, with lemonade and ginger ale to wash it all down.

As they began to eat, Rat's friend, Otter, climbed up out of the river. Rat introduced Otter and Mole, and they all had a merry lunch together. Otter and Rat told Mole how lively and fun life on the river was all year round.

Mole spotted a patch of dark woodland beyond the river and asked what it was.

"That's the Wild Wood," said Rat, as
Otter shuddered a little.

"Is it a nice place?" Mole asked.

"It's not the place that's the problem;
it's the animals," said Otter.

Rat nodded. "We riverbankers avoid
the Wild Wood. Of course, our friend
Badger lives there, but there are weasels
and stoats, too. Nasty creatures, all of
them. Stay away from the Wild Wood."

When they had finished eating, Otter said goodbye and dived back into the water. Mole and Rat packed everything up and put it in the boat. Rat began to row down the river once more.

"Rat, can I try rowing?" Mole asked.

Rat chuckled. "It's not as easy as it looks. Better wait until you know the river a little better."

Mole felt annoyed by this. How hard could rowing be? He stood up suddenly and snatched the oars from Rat. Rat was so surprised that he fell off his seat

backward. Mole tried to dig the oars
into the water and pull, but he missed
completely and ended up toppling over.
As he tried to scramble up, he slipped
and tumbled over the side of the boat,
landing in the river with a splash.

Mole couldn't swim, so he sank down
in the cold water until a brown paw came
down after him and scooped him out.
Rat plonked him on the riverbank.

"R-Rat, I'm s-so s-sorry," Mole said,
through chattering teeth.

"That's all right,"
said Rat. "Why don't
you come and stay
with me, if you like
the river? We'll
make a rower
of you yet!"

One day, when Mole had been staying at Rat's for a while, Rat announced that they were going to visit his friend, Toad.

"I'll warn you, though," said Rat, "Toad's a nice animal, but he's too rich for his own good. He's always taking up expensive hobbies for a week or so and then getting bored with them. He's tried rowing and punting and sailing. I've heard he has a new hobby now, but goodness knows what it is."

They rowed up the river to Toad Hall, a grand old house. Toad was standing outside it, and he looked delighted when he spotted them.

"Hello, hello!" he called. "You're just in time to join me on my trip!"

"Trip?" asked Rat. "Down the river, you mean?"

"Oh, pooh to the river!" Toad bounced ahead of them, leading them to a canary yellow caravan that was hitched to a horse. He flung his arms wide. "I travel by road now! The open road, in my beautiful caravan!"

"So, that's his new hobby," muttered Rat.

"You must come with me," said Toad. "I won't take no for an answer."

"It does sound rather fun," said Mole.

The next morning, they were trundling down a quiet lane. Mole was walking in front of the caravan, chatting to the horse. Toad was telling Rat stories about himself, which he loved doing.

Suddenly, they heard a buzzing noise and then a "Poop-poop!" behind them. A bright red motor car zoomed past like it was on a racetrack. It gave the horse such a fright that he leaped backward. Toad was sent flying, and the caravan fell into the ditch with a crash.

"It's broken, completely broken!" Rat shouted, while shaking his fist at the car. Mole calmed the horse down and unhitched him. Then, they both tried to pull the battered caravan out of the ditch.

"Toad, come and help," said Rat. He looked round to see Toad, sat in the

middle of the road where he had landed.
Toad looked happy as he gazed after the
car. "Poop-poop!" he said.

"What?" asked Mole.

"*That*, my friends, is the only way to
travel!" said Toad.

"I think we just discovered Toad's next
hobby," Mole whispered to Rat.

Sure enough, the next day, Toad
ordered a brand-new motor car.

CHAPTER 2
The Wild Wood

Winter arrived at the river, and it became a quiet place for once. All the animals tucked themselves away from the cold in their snug homes. It was too chilly to mess around on the water.

Rat liked to pass his days in front of the fire, writing poetry and dozing. Mole found it rather boring and longed for something to do. He remembered hearing about Rat's friend, Badger, who lived in the Wild Wood. Every animal spoke very highly of Badger, but he hadn't visited the river all summer.

"Rat, why don't we call on Badger today? I would love to meet him," Mole suggested one crisp morning.

"Not a good idea," yawned Rat, as he poured his tea. "Badger sees people only when he wants to. I'm his friend, and I've never even called on him. Besides, you don't  want to go to the Wild Wood at this time of year. It's an awful, dark place."

Mole was disappointed by this. He had left his underground home for excitement, not sitting! That

 afternoon, when Rat had begun to doze in his armchair, Mole sneaked out. "I'm not scared of any wood," he muttered to himself.

Mole scurried toward the Wild Wood in the chilly air. The bare trees and bushes were rough and tangled. "But there's nothing so scary about them," Mole muttered to himself. Inside the wood, though, the light was much dimmer than outside. The farther he went, the darker it got. The trees loomed closer and closer. Mole began to feel a little scared …

Then, Mole saw a pair of sharp eyes staring at him from a hole. Nervously, he sped up. Another mean face glared out of a small hole, then another and another.

Next, he heard pitter-pattering, as if hundreds of tiny paws were heading toward him. Mole panicked and started to run, tripping over roots in his haste to get away. He found a hollow in an old tree to hide in. Curled up, he listened to all the terrible noises outside and shivered.

"Oh, why didn't I listen to Rat?" Mole whispered sadly to himself.

Meanwhile, Rat had woken up to find Mole gone. When he spotted Mole's paw prints, he raced straight after his friend. He eventually found Mole in his hollow and crawled in. Both friends were so tired that they fell asleep.

They woke up a
few hours later to
find that a thick,
white blanket
covered the whole

wood. Snow! And it was still falling hard.

"We must try to get home," said Rat,
"but this snow makes everything look so
different, I can't be sure of the way."

After walking for a long time and not
finding the edge of the wood, they started
to lose hope of getting home. Suddenly,
Mole tumbled forward and squealed.

"Ouch, my leg! I tripped over
something—something that was hidden
in the snow!"

Rat knelt down to look at Mole's leg.
"Hmm, it's a clean cut," he said. "It looks
like something sharp did it, not a tree root."

"Well, it hurts, whatever it was," grumbled Mole.

Rat looked thoughtful and started digging through the snow.

"It's a door scraper!" he said.

"How odd!" Mole exclaimed.

Rat kept on digging. Next, a shabby old doormat appeared.

"What on earth?" cried Mole, but Rat hadn't finished. He started scraping at a bank of snow above the

doormat. The snow
fell away to reveal
a green door.

Peering close,
Mole could see a
brass plaque with
a name written on
it: Mr. Badger!

Eagerly, Rat and Mole rang the doorbell. After a while, they heard muffled shuffling and grumbling. The door swung open, and Badger peered out grumpily. "Who wants what in this weather?" he snapped.

"Please, Badger, it's us," said Rat, "We got lost in the woods."

Badger's face softened right away. "Rat and Mole! Come in, you poor, cold fellows. It's not a night for small creatures to be out." He ushered them in, and they followed him to a warm and snug kitchen.

Badger urged them to sit as he bustled around, fetching them dry clothes, hanging their wet things in front of the fire, and making a splendid supper.

Once they had eaten and shared their news, Badger asked after Toad. "Keeping out of mischief, I hope?" he said.

"Afraid not," said Rat, "He's smashed up six cars so far."

"Been in hospital three times," Mole put in.

"And has a mountain of fines to pay," Rat finished.

Badger looked very cross indeed. "Somebody needs to tell that Toad off. When the weather is warmer, I am coming over, and we will deal with him together."

Rat and Mole slept very well in Badger's comfy house and awoke only at noon, when Otter came looking for them. Badger grunted at another uninvited guest, but he made them all a delicious lunch of hot soup and fresh bread.

"Thank you for taking such good care of us, Badger, old chap," said Rat, as he wiped his whiskers. "Now, we really must be going before it gets dark again."

"Don't you worry about that," rumbled Badger, "I can take you right to the edge of the wood in my tunnels."

They followed Badger through the dark tunnels. Being underground made Mole miss his own little house for a moment, but then he shook himself. He preferred the river life, of course. Finally, they saw daylight. Badger pulled the undergrowth aside to reveal that they were at the edge of the Wild Wood.

"Run along, now," he said, "I'll see you in the summer, and we'll deal with silly Toad."

"Bye, Badger!" they chorused and set off toward the river.

When Mole glanced back, Badger had already replaced the bushes, and the tunnel had completely disappeared.

CHAPTER 3

Toad's Lesson

Badger was as good as his word. On the first proper day of summer, the sun was shining brightly on the rushing river. Mole and Rat were preparing their boat to go on a fishing trip, when Badger appeared.

"Hello there!" they cried.

Badger's face was grim. "I have heard that Toad is having a new car delivered today," he said. "We must go at once to Toad Hall."

The three friends set off along the riverbank. Sure enough, when they reached Toad Hall, a new car was sitting outside. As they drew close, the front door of Toad Hall flew open, and Toad stepped out, dressed in his driving cap and goggles.

He caught sight of them and beamed. "My good fellows! Do you like my new car? You're just in time to join me on a very jolly trip!" He faltered as he caught sight of their stern faces. "Why, whatever is the matter?"

Badger strode up the steps. "Take Toad back inside," he said to Rat and Mole. Then, he turned to the man who was delivering the car. "I'm afraid Toad does not want this car. Please take it away."

Toad spluttered and struggled as Rat and Mole dragged him through the front door. "What is the meaning of this? Let go of me! I'm going driving, you nincompoops!"

"No, you aren't," growled Badger. "You've been a fool, wasting the money your good father left you and being a danger to yourself and all the other animals. It's time somebody stopped you."

He took Toad by the shoulder and led him into the dining room, closing the door behind them.

They were in there for a long time. Rat and Mole settled into armchairs by the fire. Through the door, they could hear the growl of Badger's voice, scolding, and the squeak of Toad's voice, pleading.

Eventually, the door opened, and Toad appeared, looking very sorry for himself.

"Now," said Badger, "Toad has agreed that he will stop this driving nonsense and be a good animal once more. Haven't you, Toad? Come on, tell them what you told me."

Toad was quiet for a moment, then he burst out laughing. "No, I haven't, and I won't!" he chortled. "I love driving, and I will never stop—never!"

Badger looked furious. "Then you leave us no choice, you very silly animal."

Mole and Rat took Toad to his room and locked him in.

Badger stood behind the door as Toad yelled and beat it with his fists. "It's the only way, Toad. You'll remain there until you give up your dangerous hobbies."

Toad was furious and not very nice to be around, so they all took turns watching him.

One day, when Rat was on watch, Toad turned to him, looking rather pale and wobbly, and said, "Rat, I think I am unwell, and I need a doctor."

Rat had to agree that Toad was looking rather ill, but he didn't know what to do. Badger and Mole were both out, and he knew that he shouldn't leave Toad alone.

"I really think this might be the end," Toad muttered, falling to the floor. "Ah, well, I have lived a good life."

Rat jumped up right away and ran for the doctor.

As soon as he had gone, Toad stopped being wobbly and pale. He watched from the window as Rat hurried down the road. Toad chuckled to himself, jumped up, and dressed as quickly

as he could.
He filled
his pockets
with money.
Then, he
tied all his
bed sheets
together,
threw them
out of the
window, and
climbed down.

Toad skipped down the road, laughing and smirking to himself.

"I am the cleverest of all Toads! They can lock me in a room, but they can't outsmart me, haha! Wonderful Toad! The best actor in the land!"

He walked for a long time, and then decided to reward himself with a fine lunch at a country inn. Before he could take a bite, he heard the noise he had been dreaming of: a loud "Poop-poop!" and the rumble of a car engine. Toad leaned to look out of the window and saw a gleaming green sports car pulling up in front of the inn. The passengers all got out and came inside.

"There would be no harm in looking at it," Toad said to himself, leaving his lunch and heading outside.

"There would be no harm in starting it," Toad reasoned, cranking the handle and making the engine roar once more.

"There would be no harm in sitting in it," Toad muttered, glancing around before slipping into the leather seats.

Before he knew it, he was in the car, racing away at high speed.

"No harm! No harm at all!" Toad shrieked as the wind whooshed past him, "I am *me* again!"

Later that afternoon, Toad was in handcuffs, standing in front of a judge in court. A policeman was holding him still, and Toad kept trying to stamp on his foot.

The judge frowned down at Toad from the bench. "It is rare that we have such a dreadful and bad criminal brought before us. Now I will give you your sentence: one year in prison for stealing a valuable car. Then, I will add three years for dangerous

driving. Another *fifteen* years for being rude to a policeman, which all together would be nineteen years. So, why don't we round it up to twenty years, to be on the safe side?"

"Excellent!" said the policeman.

"Absolutely not!" gasped Toad.

"Twenty years in prison it is," said the judge. "Take him away!"

Toad could barely believe what he was hearing. He shrieked and struggled as the policeman hauled him away. Outside, the crowd threw rotten vegetables at him.

The policeman dragged him to the jail, and Toad was thrown in the deepest, darkest dungeon of the most secure prison in all of England. Toad threw himself down in his horrible cell and cried and cried.

CHAPTER 4

A Grand Escape

"Oh, this is the end of Toad! Woe is me! How stupid I have been! Why didn't I listen to wise Badger, stout Mole, and good Rat? Now I shall rot in this hole."

Toad wailed like this day and night and refused all food and drink.

The jailer's daughter was a sweet girl, who loved animals and hated that Toad was so upset. She persuaded her father to let her take Toad his meals and see if she could cheer him up. The jailer was tired of all the noise, so he agreed.

The girl took a stack of hot, buttered toast and two mugs of tea to the dungeon. "Toad, why don't you share supper with me?" she called over his crying.

Toad wanted to ignore her, but then the warm, buttery smell drifted into his nostrils, and he licked his lips.

"Very well, then, I suppose I could have a little piece of toast," he sniffed.

Soon, Toad had gobbled up nearly the entire stack of toast and drunk all the tea. He was almost back to his old self, as he told the girl tales of his life.

The girl visited Toad every day and grew fond of him. She thought it wasn't fair that he was in prison for such a long time.

"Toad," she said to her friend one day. "I think I may have a way for you to escape."

"What is it?" cried Toad, eagerly.

"My aunt is the washerwoman here," said the girl. "She is going to deliver the clean washing tomorrow. I think I could persuade her to lend you some of her clothes, and you could leave the prison disguised as her. You both have very similar figures."

Toad spluttered. "I could not leave the prison as a washerwoman!"

"Well, then, you can stay here as a toad, you ungrateful creature," said the girl.

Toad quickly understood this might be his only chance of escape. "I mean, of course, that is an excellent plan and most kind of you. It would be my pleasure to dress up as your aunt, the washerwoman."

"Wonderful!" said the girl, "I'll ask her."

Her aunt agreed, and the next day, they dressed Toad up in her clothes.

"There, nobody would know the difference!" said the girl, proudly.

Toad felt very silly, but he bit his tongue.

Toad picked up a basket of washing and made his way out of the prison. He was terrified that the guards would see through the disguise. Instead, they held the prison door open for him. They wished him a pleasant afternoon as he stepped into the fresh air.

"I am a cunning and brilliant Toad!" he whispered to himself, as he scurried down the road, completely forgetting that it hadn't been his own plan.

He ran straight to the train station to catch the fastest train home, but when he tried to pay for a ticket, he found he had no money. He'd left it in the pockets of his own clothes back at the prison!

Toad stood on the platform, cursing his bad luck. The kindly train driver spotted him and asked what was the matter.

"Oh, I am a tired, unhappy, old washerwoman, with no money to get home," Toad cried.

"You poor thing!" said the driver, "I can't just leave you here. Tell you what, how about a free ride if you do some of my washing later?"

Toad could hardly believe his luck. "That would be wonderful, kind sir. Thank you!"

The train set off in a great cloud of
steam and began to race through the
countryside. Toad smiled to himself.
He would be home in time for supper.

Then, the train driver frowned as
he looked out of the cab. "It looks like
we are being followed by
another train. A very
strange one, packed
with policemen, all
shouting 'Stop! Stop!'"

Toad suddenly felt
very scared. He fell
to his knees, shaking.
"Oh, Mr. Train Driver,
I am afraid I have not been honest with
you. I am not a simple washerwoman. I am
the Famous Toad. I just escaped from the
horrid dungeon that my enemies threw

me in, and now they are trying to catch me again. Please, won't you help me?"

The train driver looked thoughtful. "I think you must be a very bad Toad, but I feel sorry for you. So, I will help."

Together, they scooped coal in the train's stove, so they could pick up speed. But no matter how fast they went, the train of policemen kept catching up with them.

"It's no good!" said the train driver. "They're faster than us."

"Oh, what shall I do?" shrieked Toad.

"Listen," said the driver, "we are about to go through a tunnel." He pointed to it up ahead. "We will come out of the other end while they are still inside. That's your chance. You will have to jump for it before they come out. They won't see you, and they can keep on chasing my train until I run out of coal."

Toad gulped. The train was going so fast, he didn't know how hard his landing would be, but he nodded.

The train shot into the tunnel. Everything went black, and the sound was almost deafening. When they came out the other side, Toad saw that a bank sloped steeply down to a dark wood.

The driver shouted, "JUMP!"

Toad leaped from the train and tumbled down the bank. Luckily, it didn't

hurt. He jumped up and ran to the
trees. From his hiding place, he saw the
policemen's train rattle past, with all of
them still shouting, "Stop!"

Toad laughed heartily to himself. He
was free! Then, he remembered he was
also all alone in a strange, dark wood.
Feeling a little scared, he found a hollow
tree, curled up inside, and went to sleep.

CHAPTER 5

Homeward Bound

The next morning dawned bright and cheerful. Toad woke up in his hollow. For a moment, he had no idea where he was—or why he was wearing a dress! Then, the story of his daring escape came back to him.

"That's right! I am a free Toad!" he giggled. He leaped out of the hollow and set off to try and find the way home.

Before too long, he came across a pathway by a canal. An old horse was pulling a brightly painted canal barge. There was a stout woman at the back, steering the boat.

She greeted Toad. "Lovely morning, isn't it?"

Toad put on his best washerwoman voice. "Maybe it is for those who aren't in trouble, like me. Here I am, a poor washerwoman, called to help my poor daughter, but now I'm lost, and I've got no money. Goodness knows how I will reach her now. She lives by Toad Hall."

"Well, I'm going that way myself!" said the woman. "This canal joins the river up there, and then it's only a short walk to Toad Hall. Why don't I take you?"

Toad climbed onto the barge, congratulating himself again for being so clever. He settled down next to the barge woman, and they chatted as the boat drifted lazily along.

"Do you enjoy being a washerwoman?" asked the barge woman.

"Enjoy? Why, there's nothing I love more in the world," lied Toad.

"Oh, well then, I have a treat for you!" smiled the barge woman. She pulled out a huge pile of dirty clothes. "I hate washing, and these are terribly dirty. You can wash them. It's my gift to you!"

Toad couldn't see a way out of it, even though he had no idea how to wash

clothes. He took them to the tub she
pointed to, dunked them in the water,
and rubbed them, but nothing seemed to
get them clean. Toad got
hot, cross,
and covered
in soapsuds.

"I'm afraid
there's something
wrong with your
washtub," he said.

"I'm afraid there's something wrong
with *you*," retorted the barge woman.
"You're no washerwoman!"

Toad stood up and kicked the tub. "That
is true. I am the world famous Toad."

"Yuck, a toad!" the barge woman
squealed. She picked him up and threw
him into the river.

Toad landed with a big splash in the chilly water. Brrr, it was cold and full of slimy duckweed. He tried to swim for the shore but was slowed down by his wet dress.

The barge woman was laughing so hard at him that tears were streaming down her face. "Take that, you nasty Toad!" she called, as she sailed off.

Toad was determined to get even. He struggled to the bank and pulled himself up onto dry land. Then, he gathered up his wet skirts and raced after the barge. Catching up with the plodding horse, he jumped on its back. Then, he cut the tow rope and cantered off, leaving the barge far behind.

It was Toad's turn to laugh as the barge woman waved her arms and cursed him.

"Take that!" he yelled back at her.

He rode several miles on the horse
before meeting a man who was making a
delicious-smelling breakfast. Toad's tummy
rumbled, and he gave the horse to the
man in return for some food and money.

Toad walked on, feeling very smug with
how things had turned out. As he walked,
he made up a song about his adventures.

Toad caught sight of a car and clapped his hands in delight.

"Oh, what a stroke of luck!" he cried, "I shall ask them for a lift and that excellent car will take me all the way home. I can't wait to see Badger's face!"

He stepped out into the middle of the road and waved at the car.

But as it drew closer, Toad's glee turned to horror. The car approaching was the very same one that he had stolen from outside the inn!

Toad was certain he would be taken straight back to prison if they saw it was him. He was so scared that his legs felt weak, and he slumped down in the middle of the road.

He heard the car stop and two men getting out.

"Oh, dear, that poor woman must have fainted in the heat," said one of them.

"Let's take her to the nearest village and see if anyone knows her," said the other.

Gently, they picked Toad up and laid him in the back seat. As they drove away, Toad felt the roar of the engine beneath him and his courage came back. He just couldn't help himself …

Toad sat up and said in a wavering voice, "Good sirs, I think I might feel better if I could sit at the front, next to the driver."

The kind men stopped the car, moved Toad to the front seat, and set off again.

A few minutes later, Toad said, "Why, I should love to try driving this car. I've been watching you, and I believe I could do it."

The men laughed and the driver said, "I like your spirit. Go on, try it."

They shuffled seats again, and Toad slammed his foot down, making the car zoom off.

"Slow down!" cried the driver.

Toad cackled. "Never! 'Tis I, the famous, fearless Toad!"

"It's the wretch who stole our car! Get him!" said the men.

They tried to grab the steering wheel from Toad, but he shoved them back, and the car spun off the road and into a hedge. Toad went flying through the air and landed straight in the river! It was flowing very fast, and Toad was whisked along, spinning and dipping below the surface several times until he drifted up against a bank. There, he found himself looking up at a familiar face. It was Rat!

CHAPTER 6

The Battle for Toad Hall

"My good Rat!" Toad cried, as Rat fished him out of the river. "I have had such an adventure. You will never believe what a clever Toad I have been. It all began with my daring escape from the deepest, darkest dungeon—"

"Oh, do be quiet, Toad," said Rat, looking a bit cross. "Come and change into dry clothes, or you'll catch a cold."

Toad followed Rat to his house and

changed. Then, Rat laid out sandwiches for lunch.

"Now," said Toad, "I shall tell you my splendid stories. Where to begin? How about the time I leaped like a daredevil from a speeding train? Or stole a mean old barge woman's horse?"

Rat glared at Toad. "Stop it this minute. Those stories don't sound splendid. They sound ridiculous and embarrassing. Stealing horses? You are an idiot, Toad, and you have been ever since you bought that first car."

Toad was shocked, but he knew there was some truth to what Rat said. After a moment, he replied. "You are right, Rat. I have been a fool. I will go home right away and get rid of all my cars."

"Home?" cried Rat. "You can't go home! Haven't you heard?"

"Heard what?" Toad asked.

"Why, the weasels have taken Toad Hall for themselves!" said Rat.

Toad frowned. "Impossible."

"I tell you, they have," Rat insisted. "When you were arrested, the riverbankers were all on your side and said it was a terrible thing, but the Wild Wood creatures said you deserved it. Mole and Badger decided to move into Toad Hall, to take care of it until you returned."

"They are, indeed, excellent friends," said Toad.

"But one dark, stormy night, the weasels broke in to Toad Hall, beat poor Badger and Mole, and threw them out! Toad,

I'm afraid the weasels have been living in your house ever since."

Toad was almost shaking with fury. He pushed his chair back and said, "Well, it's time I kicked them out again!"

Rat said, "Toad, wait!"

But Toad was already out of the door and marching to Toad Hall. There was a nasty weasel standing guard at the door.

"This is my house!" Toad said to him. "I demand that you all leave immediately!"

The weasel grinned as he pointed a gun at Toad and pulled the trigger.

Toad yelped and dived.

"I tried to tell you," Rat said when Toad returned, a little shaken. "We'll need a proper plan to take it back. Let's wait for Badger and Mole to get home. They've been camping out, watching Toad Hall."

Soon, Badger and Mole appeared, looking tired and dirty. They greeted Toad with weary joy.

"Although it isn't much of a homecoming without a home," said Badger.

"How will we take it back?" Toad asked.

"It's a hopeless situation," moaned Mole. "They have dozens of armed sentries posted at every entrance. When they see us watching, they just laugh."

"Oh, hopeless indeed," murmured Rat.

Toad began to wail at the thought of never getting his home back.

"Silence!" roared Badger. "Toad Hall is thoroughly guarded, it's true. But I know a secret passageway that opens up in the middle of it."

"There is no such thing!" Toad declared.

"Indeed, there is," said Badger, "in the butler's pantry. Your father never told you because he knows you can't keep a secret. The weasels are holding a banquet for the Chief Weasel's birthday tomorrow night. So, they'll be unarmed and distracted. We can sneak through the passageway and take them by surprise."

"Where is Mole?" Rat asked the next morning. Nobody had seen him.

At that moment, Mole trotted up, wearing Toad's old washerwoman dress. "I've just been down to Toad Hall," he giggled. "I pretended to be a washerwoman looking for work. I told the sentries that I'd heard hundreds of badgers, rats, moles, and toads were coming from all directions to attack Toad Hall tonight! They all started panicking!"

"Excellent work, Mole," said Badger, heartily. "They'll be so worried about what's coming from outside, they won't be prepared for anything coming from the inside. You clever creature!"

When night fell, the friends armed themselves with big sticks and set off, with Badger leading. They took the secret passageway and slipped up through the trapdoor. The weasels were all laughing and singing in the next room, enjoying Toad's finest food and wine.

The Chief Weasel stood up on his chair. "I would like to declare a toast to Mr. Toad, our host. Long may he rot in jail, so that we can enjoy his house!"

The weasels all roared with laughter. Badger turned and nodded to the others.

"NOW!"

They burst into the banquet room, yelling. For a moment, the weasels just stared in shock. Then they leaped up, smashing plates and glasses. The huge table was overturned, and chairs went flying.

A great fight began. The weasels had their fists and teeth, but they were no match for the big sticks that the four friends carried.

Toad went straight for the Chief Weasel and gave him a few good whacks with his stick. "Have me rot in jail, would you?" Toad shouted. "Take that and that!"

The Chief Weasel squealed in pain and dived out of the window.

Meanwhile, Badger was picking weasels up and hurling them toward the door. Rat had forgotten his stick and was wrestling with a couple of weasels by the fireplace. Mole was chasing shrieking weasels as they escaped through the doors, the windows, and even up the chimney!

In a few minutes, the room was cleared. "We've won!" cried Toad.

Through the windows, they could see the weasels racing out so fast that they all ended up falling in the river. Toad was master of the Hall once more!

"I think another banquet would be just the thing to celebrate," Badger suggested, "but with no speeches or songs by Toad."

"Oh," said Toad, crestfallen.

Toad did finally learn his lesson that day. He became humble and did not boast about himself any longer. The other animals liked him all the better for it.

The weasels had learned their lesson, too. They would never hurt the friends of Badger, Mole, Rat, and Toad. All creatures could walk around the Wild Wood safely.